Enny Penny
and the
Mermaid

written by Erin Lee
illustrated by Ishan Trivedi

to my mom

E.L.

Enny Penny is a little girl with big wishes. Every night before going to sleep she makes a wish. Tonight she is thinking about her beach vacation!

"I wish to build the
best sandcastle ever!"

Then Enny Penny falls fast asleep.

The next day after three hundred songs, twenty one games of I Spy, fifteen bathroom breaks and sixty-six knock-knock jokes...

"YEAH! I'm going to build the best sandcastle ever!" said Enny Penny.

"We made it! Everyone out of the car!" Dad yells.

"Pails, shovels, buckets, rake...
Jared, what's this?"
Enny Penny asked.

"That's my Secret Stealthy
Samurai hat. I've been
looking for that! I'm off to
find Ninja Stars," said Jared.

"Let's go kids!"
Mom yells.

The building of the *best sandcastle ever* gets
interrupted by a very dark, very scary storm cloud.
"Oh no! My sandcastle is getting ruined!"
"I will have to start all over!" said Enny Penny.

The next day, Enny Penny is ready.
"It's a beautiful day to build a sandcastle!" said Enny Penny.

"I'm on the hunt for Ninja Stars," said Jared.

"My sandcastle is looking marvelous," said Enny Penny.

"It's almost finished!"

Enny Penny put the finishing touches on her sandcastle

"The waves! They've erased my sandcastle!
I have to start all over, AGAIN."

"Shake it off, shake it off. I can do this!"
Enny Penny said as she filled her bucket with water.

But no sooner than
Enny Penny gets started...

"NO! Jared!

Stop feeding the birds.
They are destroying my
sandcastle!"

"That's it! I quit! I'm not building my sandcastle all over, AGAIN," Enny Penny said as she picked up her board and headed out to the water.

"Whoa! What is that?"
said Enny Penny.

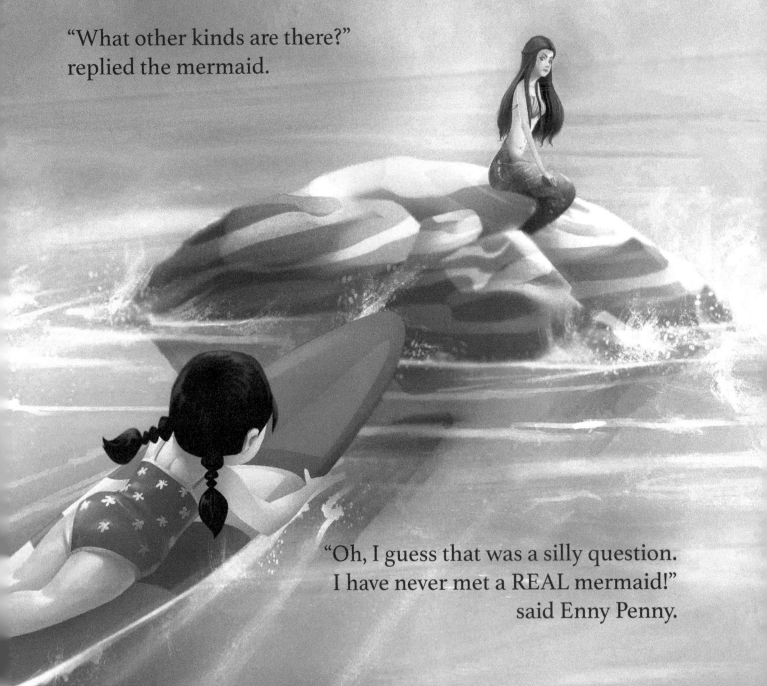

"Are you a REAL mermaid?"
asked Enny Penny.

"What other kinds are there?"
replied the mermaid.

"Oh, I guess that was a silly question.
I have never met a REAL mermaid!"
said Enny Penny.

"You look sad dear. Is there something I can help you with?" asked the mermaid.

"I want to build the *best sandcastle* ever! I've had to start over three times. My brother and the ocean keep messing it up." said Enny Penny.

"Well dear, the beauty of the ocean is that with every wave it takes away something old and brings something new," said the mermaid.

"How is that going to help me?" Enny Penny asked as the beautiful mermaid disappeared into the ocean.

Enny Penny starts building the *best sandcastle* ever all over, again.

But this time the weather cooperates...

...Jared and the birds stay away.

...and the tide stayed out.

"That's it!
I'm finished—but
something is missing."

"Enny Penny, look what
I found! It's a **Ninja Star!**"

"Jared, that's it!"
said Enny Penny.

"Now that's the *best sandcastle ever!*"

"What an amazing sandcastle.
Good job, Enny Penny!" said Dad.

"Enny Penny, this is the best
sandcastle you have ever made!
It must have been very difficult
to build," said Mom.

"It was VERY hard to build, but I had a little
help from the ocean, a mermaid and Jared,"
Enny Penny said. "Dad, hurry and take the picture
before my sandcastle gets washed away!"

CPSIA information can be obtained
at www.ICGtesting.com
Printed in the USA
BVHW021700250220
573162BV00020B/1167